*To my son, Zac, who is never afraid to "BEE" himself.*
~ Dave

Text and illustrations © 2014 Dave Whamond

Owlkids Books acknowledges the financial support of the Canada Council for the Arts, the Ontario Arts Council, the Government of Canada through the Canada Book Fund (CBF) and the Government of Ontario through the Ontario Media Development Corporation's Book Initiative for our publishing activities.

Published in Canada by
Owlkids Books Inc.
10 Lower Spadina Avenue
Toronto, ON M5V 2Z2

Published in the United States by
Owlkids Books Inc.
1700 Fourth Street
Berkeley, CA 94710

Library and Archives Canada Cataloguing in Publication

Whamond, Dave, author, illustrator
     Oddrey joins the team / written and illustrated by Dave Whamond.

ISBN 978-1-77147-061-2 (bound)

     I. Title.

PS8645.H34O35 2014       jC813'.6       C2014-900167-3

Library of Congress Control Number: 2014931865

Edited by: Jennifer Stokes
Designed by: Barb Kelly

Manufactured in Shenzhen, China, in March 2014, by C&C Joint Printing Co.
Job #HO0637

A       B       C       D       E       F

Publisher of Chirp, chickaDEE and OWL
www.owlkidsbooks.com

# Oddrey

## Joins the Team

Written and illustrated by

# DAVE WHAMOND

Owl
kids

Oddrey loved sports. Sometimes she even liked to make up her own.

BOINGY
OINGY

So when her friend Maybelline asked her to join the school soccer team, Oddrey decided she'd give it a try.

Oddrey played soccer a bit differently than the other kids on the team. At her first practice with the Piccadilla Bees, she showed everyone her stuff.

Her soccer coach said she had interesting technique.

Her teammates said they liked her unique practice drills.

Oddrey herself simply knew that there was more than one way to get the job done.

BIP

Maybelline was the Piccadilla Bees' star player. Her drop kicks were amazing. And she could expertly dribble, volley, and lob the ball from one end of the field to the other.

The big game against the Quagville Crushers was coming up, and Maybelline was determined that each Bee would be ready.

JUST KICK IT!

HI-YA!

Milton worked on his karate kick.

LESS SPINNING!

Trish developed her breakaway cartwheels.

Oddrey tried to master some of Maybelline's winning soccer moves.

But they just didn't feel right.

Then, on the day of the big game, *nothing* felt right. Despite everyone's hard work, the Bees were really struggling.

Even Maybelline couldn't score a goal.

The Bees had lost their buzz. Not even Pineapple Snack Break could lift their spirits.

Then Oddrey realized
that the team was named
the Bees for a reason.

Oddrey explained to the team that each bee in every hive has its own special job, but all the bees—drones, workers, and the queen—have to work together to make the honey.

"I don't remember anything about honey in the rule book, Oddrey," said the coach.

"Come on, coach," said Oddrey.
"Let's switch to Plan Bee!"

And so the team put Plan Bee into action. Maybelline actually passed the ball to her teammates. Oddrey danced it to the end zone. Milton karate-kicked it to Trish. Trish cartwheeled it to Earl. And Earl…

Well, Earl used his head!

The Bees didn't win that day. But they did have fun playing together.

And afterward, Oddrey wondered if everyone might like to try a new game…

"Hey, Oddrey," said one of the Quagville Crushers, "what are you playing?"

"I call it Oddball," said Oddrey. "Do you want to play, too?"